THE

MAGIC

WORLD WAR - 1

Cyscoprime Publishers

Parijat Extension, Bilaspur, Chhattisgarh 495001
First Published By Cyscoprime Publishers 2020
Copyright © Shivam Gupta 2020
All Rights Reserved.
ISBN: 978-93-90047-06-2
MRP: Rs.150/–

THE

MAGIC

WORLD WAR - 1

SHIVAM GUPTA

ABOUT THE BOOK

This is a book based on the imagination of the magical world. It is a fiction book about magics that happened in the magic world. In this book, you will get to know about the magic book found in Teblanpur. It is a suspense story you will get to know how it came in Teblanpur, and about Mavish who works as a protector of the magic book. There are 10 parts and each part is very interesting to read. If you will read then you will feel that you are watching Hollywood adventurous movie. It is very adventurous to read.

ABOUT THE AUTHOR

Shivam Kumar Gupta, born in Garhwa district village Bishunpura, education started from Nagar Utari, studied in Kinder garden educational complex which is a primary school. There he studied till class 4 and left it in 2014. After that, he was admitted to Daltonganj in St.mariam's school in 2015. It is a secondary school and still, he is studying in 8th and has been promoted to 9th in 2020.

CONTENTS

1

The mystery city

There was a place named Teblanpur. This was the place that was unknown to everyone. Even then the climate was suitable for them but the climate was not suitable for normal people. The place was located at the center of the forest where plants and animals were a friend for them. But it was surrounded by mountains around that forest. There was a river that passes through the forest and provides adequate water for survival the place was very safe from in every condition. When a leaf of the tree falls in the river it works as a medicine. The tree bear fruits in every condition throughout the year because there is a story about this. The story is that a thousand years ago it was believed that under this forest gold, diamond, and the magic book was found. The king of this place was afraid of this place. The name of the king was The Gangi. He was having four sons. But there was one feature of the king that he was having magical power. When the neighboring king gets to know that under the forest of Teblanpur there is gold, diamond, and magic book, the neighboring king announced war between king Gangi. The war lasted for more than one month. The economic condition becomes bad due to war. Many of the people died due to starvation. But the sorrow movement of the king started when four of his sons were dead. He was happy to save this place and people were buried inside the earth. The king took out the magic book from the forest of Teblanpur. To make the place very safe for these people. So, he made a dense forest around Teblanpur. And formed a high mountain around the forest. To hide the magic book. He had formed a tree which was the biggest tree of that forest. He formed a gate at the center of the tree. When you pronounced the word "KRAB", then the gate of the tree would open. Then he hides that book inside it. The king surrounded it with huge plants and trees. And the animals and trees were like a friend to them. And the forest was surrounded by a range of mountains. Now the people were surviving in a very good way. They were living happily. But after some time king died. Now no one can rule over them. The dead body of the people of war was buried inside that place converted into coal, other minerals after a thousand years. And there was a river which passes through the forest which provided water. But there was an interesting fact that when the leaves of the trees fall in that river then the water keeps them away from the diseases. And one more fact was that these trees would never dry. And it would bear fruits and flowers in every condition and season. And the mountain was too high that no one was able to look at that place. They would recognize that there is nothing after this mountain. And the place becomes a mystery for everyone. But some of the magic of king were in trees, mountain, and river. The place was a mystery for everyone.

2

The born of future

There was a poor family who lives in the Teblanpur. They were considered as low caste and were discriminated against by the people who were not equally treated. There was a boy named Mavish is born in that family. When the king was dying, he predicted that there will be a boy who will be born in a poor family. This was the time when the boy was born. When he grew up he had sacrificed his family for the low caste discrimination problem he faced many times in his childhood from the other people. Then he went to the teacher of a locality. He used to teach every people either he belongs to a low caste or upper caste. When the saint or teacher saw him then he knew that he is the only boy who will be the king of the magic book. Then the saint told him everything about the prehistory of the Teblanpur. The saint was having a magic power that is he wants to make a map any location then it was possible by him. But the map made by him was not normal to a map. It was a special map that if he doesn't know the location then he can know that location and draw on a page like a map. During his journey, if he faces some problem then he does not know that how to come out from that difficulty, then he would say that "please help me" then the solution of the difficulty automatically comes out from that map. But when he reached the tree then he could not find out the magic book. So he was returned there. Then he told the saint that I could not find the magic book. Then the saint remembered that the book was hidden at the center of the tree by the king. And there is a word when it pronounced KRAB then it would open. Then again he went to the tree. This time he succeeded to find the magic book. When he went there, then he pronounced the word KRAB and the gate was open. Then the boy opened the book. At the starting page of the book, it was written that when you click the upper corner of the page it would be converted to a ring. And it would safe from every magic of enemy. When he returns to the Teblanpur then the saint was very happy to see him. He thought that this time there was nothing wrong in the journey has occurred. Then he asked the boy that did you bring the magic book? Then the boy answered that I forget the word which was told by you. The next day while he was sleeping then the boy told the ring that please read the thought of the saint and what would happen if he gives the magical book to the saint. Then the ring said close your eyes. When the boy closes his eyes, he saw that the book was taken by saint and the saint constructed a house with the help of his magic. No one entered to that house till when the saint did not allow. With the help of his magic saint took a copy of the magic book. Then he learned all the magic from the magic book. When he did not come out, many questions were arriving in the mind of the people. After one month he came out. Now he was the king of the magic book. He targeted the Mavish and put him in the magic cage. And the property of it was that without the permission of the saint. He took the Mavish to the tree where the magic book was kept. There was the biggest and largest leave in which the cage was present along with Mavish was kept and the leave was used as a prison for Mavis.

The saint thought that Mavish will die after a long period, when he will not get food and water in the cage. But for your kind information, you had remembered that plants and animals were friends for people of that place. When the root absorbs the water and food it was transported the leave. And the leave would provide that food to Mavish. This way he was alive inside the leave. This would happen if he would give the saint the magic book. During the whole night, this was told by the ring which was a magic book.

3

The secret of saint

Mavish gets up after his deep thinking about the saint that he if he gives the magic book to the saint then what will happen. He went to the saint where he used to teach the children. Then the boy Mavish said that he has the magic book, but he did not tell the saint about it. The saint told him to give the book, but the boy did not give him. The anger can be easily seen to the saint face. After that, the saint was converted as a minister of the king Nigla. The Mavish asked the saint who is king Nigla? The saint then tells him a story. Thousand years ago when the war was going between the saint and neighboring king to take control over Teblanpur. That is because of the huge amount of gold, diamond along with the magic book which contains the world's powerful magic. If he learned all the magic then he would have control over the entire world. He would become the king of magic. But the enemy of king Gangi whose name was king Nigla, aware of the war, but he did not want to involve in the war. He was not interested because he did not know about the gold, diamonds, and the magic book of the Teblanpur. Then the boy again asked why the king Nigla do not want to involve in the war. The saint said that king Nigla was wanted to have control over the neighboring kingdoms. But he could not fight with a huge number of the king. And he was confirmed that the king Gangi would be able to defeat all the king with the help of four sons, so he did not want to involve in the war. When all the neighboring kings were defeated by the sons of Gangi. And his sons have also died in the war. Then the king Nigla had control over the kingdom of a neighboring king. Then to know the reason for the war why this war had taken place and for what. He had sent his minister as a saint in the Teblanpur. When the saint came then he talks to the king and he knew all the events which took place. And he also saw the magic book which was taken out from the ground of Teblanpur. And the saint helped him in many works of a king, so he becomes a favorite of ling Gangi. When the king was hiding that book in the tree on one went aware of this information. Only the saint was allowed to go with him. So he knew the word KRAB to open that tree. When the king was dying at that time the king only offered the magic of map location. No one can go outside from the Teblanpur because the mountain and forest were too high and dense which was described early in part 1. So it was named "the mystery city" which become a mystery for everyone. This was the secret of the saint. King Nigla was the king of the half kingdom of the magic world.

4

The Show War

In the war, there will be a war between the saint and Mavish. And the Mavish will get victory over the saint. He will cage him in the cage and put him in the bark of the biggest tree. When the Mavish heard the secret of the saint. Then the war between the saint and the Mavish was going to start. Before starting the war the Mavish said to the ring what to do? Then the king said that when you will say activate, the defensive magic will be generated. Then the war was going between the saint and the Mavish in the battleground of war, the war was going for a long time.

During the first time, Mavish was unable to have control on the magic of saint. Then the Mavish said activate. The defensive magic started and it protected the Mavish from the powerful magic of saint. And the war lasted for one week. He got victory over the saint. The saint was alive. He did not want to defeat him because when the magic world war will happen then the saint will fight from king Nigla. Then the Mavish said to the ring that please take out the world's hardest diamond from the ground of the Teblanpur. The ring made contradicted a cage made up of diamond. It was used as a prison for the saint. According to the thought of the saint and punishment gave to Mavish which is described in the secret of the saint in part 3. So he put the saint in the cage. Before putting the saint in the cage. He said to the ring that takes out all the magic the magic of map. And the Mavish took all the magic including the magic of map. Again he put him inside the cage. And he took him to the biggest tree where the magic book was hidden, in the thought when the ring told Mavish that saint has put him in the biggest leave described in the part3. But the Mavish was getting food and water. But he wanted that he should put the saint into the bark of the tree where the water and food were not available. And the bark is the part of the tree which is dry. But Mavish does not want that he should die because in the two magic world war the saint will play an important role from king Nigla. If he will not get food and water then also he can survive for war. The ground where the war between the saint and Mavish took place. That ground was known by the name "battleground of raw". This was the short war so it is named "the show war".

5

The king of magic book

After the show war which is named as a battleground of the raw. There was no one to disturb him. But in the future, if some powerful magician king came to fight with him. Then what will happen? If the ring will unable to safe at any wrong moment. Then the control over to the magic book would be by another one. And the magic world can be in danger. So he said the ring to convert into the magic book. The ring said that when you will pronounce the word KRAB. Then the ring will be converted into the magic book. Again he said to the ring that finds a suitable place to pronounce the word where no one can come, the king replied that the safest place where no one can arrive is only the top of the mountain which is too high to climb, and the mountain looks like the model of Mount Everest. Then the boy said to the ring that does something that no one can see me. Then the ring constructed a circle that looks like a ball of fire. The circle was too shiny and looks like the light of the sun. That light creates an illusion that there are light beams that come from the sun.

At the starting of the story, I forget to tell that the boy told to the people of Teblanpur that he is going on a journey of Teblanpur and wants to know about the height of the mountain. And this was the excuse made by him to go on the mountain. There the Mavish was learning and remembering all the magic and he was doing the experiment and knowing how to use the magic book. There he learned all the magic from the magic book. And the fact about the magic world was that if anyone can learn all the magic of magic book then he became the king of the magic book as well as the king of the magic world. This book contains all the powerful magic to defeat the world's powerful magical kings and the king of the magic book will be able to get victory over any battle which will take place in the future. There he had spent more than five months in learning and remembering the magic of the magic book. Instead of there all magic he also got the magic map of and magic of invisible car which will play an important role in the magic world war I. he took the three too copy of the magic book. One magic book he hides in the biggest tree which will be opened by pronouncing the word KRAB. Then he clicked the corner of the second book and the book was converted into the ring and he wears it. The third book he kept inside his mind in the form of words. Now he became the king of the magic book as we discussed earlier. Now he has no fear of anyone.

THE MAGIC WORLD WAR - 1

6

The World Journey

As the Mavish became the king of the magic world as well as the magic book. Then he was the king of the world. The people of the world were citizens of the magic world, so there is the responsibility of the Mavish to look after them. So he went on the journey to the world to see the condition of people that what the condition is after Teblanpur?

To go from Teblanpur he has passed from a dense forest and high mountain. Now he was out of Teblanpur. During his journey, he was feeling thirsty so he went to the bank of the river to drink water. He drank the water but he heard somebody crying. At the bank of the river far away from that he saw a beautiful girl. She was so beautiful that her beauty cannot be described in the words. Then the Mavish asked her who are you? She said that I am the daughter of king Dashwood and my name is Aurial. She also asked with the boy and he replied that I am Mavish and I am the king of the magic book and magic world. Again the king asked her the reason of her crying, then she replied that a few days before there was a scarcity of food and many people were suffering from the diseases. She said that there is a kingdom of a word that is neighboring to king Nigla, but when I went for help to him, he behaved in a very wrong way and he did not help me. He was coming behind me however I saved my life. My father has magic of disappearing then my father gave me which was located in the crown of my head. So I used the magic and disappeared. I came here and was crying for help. Then the Mavish told me that I want to go in your kingdom and see the condition of the people. But there was a condition, that there was a magical Casio from which four words came out and the person who will be able to make suitable sentences can only enter that kingdom. So the king Nigla did not get victory on the kingdom of the word. Then the

Mavish told the magic book of the word that kept in his mind converted the four words into suitable sentences "the word of plant and animal". There he went to the kingdom of the word and he said to king Dashwood that if I will save your people from the scarcity of food and disease, you will have to permit to marry your daughter Aurial. The king accepted that said yes I will do so. After that Mavish said to the Aurial that if she gives him the magic to disappear then he will give her jubilee diamonds during the marriage ceremony. Then the king Dashwood become the friend of Mavish and he promised that he will help Mavish during the magic world war I. then the Mavish went to his kingdom Teblanpur. There he took all the fruits from the magical tree which bear fruits in every season and condition. He also took the medical water in which the leaves of trees fall then the water becomes the medical water. Then he went to the kingdom of the word where he gave the fruits as food and the medical water. After one week the condition was normal. Now the people were surviving in a good way. According to the promise done by the king Dashwood to the Mavish. Mavish marries to the daughter of King Dashwood Aurial.

During the marriage ceremony, the Mavish had a jubilee diamond made of gold and diamond which was taken out from the ground of Teblanpur.

Instead of jubilee diamonds, he had taken the magic to disappear from the Aurial. He took the magic of disappearing because there is use of thin in the magic world war I. He told her that I am the king of magic book then she said that it is not possible to take the magic book because it is in the city which is a mystery for everyone. And the city has become a mystery city for everyone. Again he told everything that I am the boy who was predicated by king Gangi when he was dying. I am Mavish. Again he told the ring to change into the magic book. She understands that he is only the king of the magic book. He had given a dozen of magical trees to the king Dashwood which bears fruits in every season and any condition.

7

The golden palace

When he was returning from the kingdom of word with the queen Aurial, then both of them went to the Teblanpur. There she saw that most of the things were like a magical thing, as she saw the magical tree which bears fruits every season and in any condition. And the river, in which when leaves fall, then the water converted to medical water. She was amazed to see these all things. And the Mavish took her to the biggest tree where he had pronounced the word KRAB. She saw that the tree opened from the center of the tree. And

Mavish took out the book. Now she believing in a reality that Mavish is the king of the magical book. She was thinking like that she had come to the magic world. And the highest mountain around the Teblanpur. Then Aurial asked the Mavish that there are some doubts in her mind that who is the head of the magic book and how did it come here? And he was also shocked to listen to her question. Now the Mavish and Aurial were living together in a small house where everything was available. The Aurial never told to Mavish that she wanted to live in a palace. Then one day while he was sleeping then suddenly in his mind one thought came that I am the king of the magic book and I can live a luxury life and can look after the citizen. Since it was believed that under the ground of Teblanpur, there is a huge amount of gold and diamonds they why should not he take it out? And there is no use of these all things under the ground. Teblanpur was located in a vast area. He used his magical map so that he can know the location of gold and diamonds. Then he got the location with the help of the magic of the map. He told the ring to take out all the diamonds and gold the ring took out and gave it to him.

Now the Mavish has built a huge palace made up of gold. There was one magical power that when the light from the sun stop coming and the place will be dark then the palace will start shining. The palace can be lifted from one place to another place. At the miner, he has used the diamond at the top of the mountain because when the light from the sun will fall directly on the palace then the gold will not melt and diamond is used as an insulator which is used to reflect the light but not absorb it. Now the golden palace was built by him. There were four hardest diamonds then he thought these diamonds are so sharp that if someone will touch it then he dies. This diamond was put on the top of the mountain at four corners. In the happiness of the golden palace, he has distributed some magic that was common in the life of the people of Teblanpur. There were large uses of that magic. The Aurial and Mavish were living a very happy life in the Golden Palace.

8

The reason for the war

When they were living happily together. Then one day the Mavish was thinking about the saint he wanted that he should take him out from the diamond cage. Then the Mavish went to the tree there he put out the saint from the bark of the tree. He took him to the golden palace. The delicious food was made for him because in the diamond cage he did not get food and water. After a long day, the saint is getting to eat food. He was alive by the blessing of Mavish that without the wish of

Mavish he will not die because when the world war will happen then he will help king Nigla. So he was alive. Then the Mavish and the saint took their dinner. Again the next morning the Mavish told to the saint look at the miner there are the diamond which works as insulators and four diamonds at four corners of the mountain.

Then after some time, he had gone to his king Nigla. Then he asked king Nigla that do you know me? King Nigla replied that he did not know him an asked who are you and what you want? He told that I don't want anything I am your minister and you had sent me to the Teblanpur during the war to know the reason for the war. But I was there from so many years, after the war, no one can come or go from the Teblanpur a dense forest and the high mountain were built whose height cannot be measurable. So I was not able to come. Now I am going to tell you the reason for the war. It was believed that under the ground of Teblanpur huge amount of diamond gold and magic book was found. So to get these all things there was the war between neighboring king and Gangi. There I was surviving in the name of a saint and he hides that magic book in the big tree when you pronounced the word KRAB it will open. The king was dead, after him the control over the Teblanpur is now in the hands of Mavish who is the king of the magic book and his wife

Aurial who is the queen of the Teblanpur. This was the reason and story of the war. But the Nigla asked that why did he send you? Then he told me that he was telling that you will help the king Nigla in the magic world war I. yes it is truly a world war which will be magical and held on the land of the magic world.

9

The Challenge War

When the saint told all the reasons for the war and about the magic book and golden palace and also about diamonds. One idea arises in the mind of king Nigla that I have captured everything, snatch the golden palace, magic book, and diamonds. He was confirmed before only that he will be able to not attack directly on the Teblanpur. To do this they have to climb the mountain to reach Teblanpur. He wrote a letter to Mavish that there will be a challenging war between us. If you are ready then reply to your answer with your signature. The letter was reached to the Mavish through eagle then he was agreed about the challenging war. And in the letter, he told that the war will be held in the sky and there he prepared a magical ground for the war which is known by the name of the ground "the ground of magical war".

After few days both of them came to each other in the sky where king Nigla told us that with the help of our magic we will make a "magical judgment" to whom you have to sacrifice your golden palace, sharper diamond, and gold present in the ground of Teblanpur. The magical judgment took all these things and by the order of king Nigla it was told that the magical judgment will hide these all things at a place that is also called "the unknown place of magic judgment" and who will be able to find these all things. First, he will take everything if he will lose then a part of the kingdom of Nigla will be taken. And the help of magic f map given by the saint was able to find the location of that place "the unknown place of magic judgment". He got the location of the place.

Again with the help of the magic of disappear, this magic of disappearing was given by Aurial instead of jubilee diamonds. And he sat on the magic of invisible car and went to the unknown place of magic judgment.

He went there and saw the magical judgment and it told that this is a page and show to the king Nigla. When he showed to king Nigla then a sound came from it that he is the winner. And according to the treaty the king Nigla had given one percent of the part of his kingdom. Let me tell you the condition of king Nigla when the game started, he started to wander here and there but he could not find that place. When he got tired he was waiting for the Mavish when he would be able to agree that I am the winner. This war was like a game but the greedy of Nigla got in the loss. The Mavish took the one percent part of the kingdom of Nigla and he gave it to king Dashwood the king of the kingdom of the word as a gift to him.

Now there was control was of Dashwood. He Dashwood told him the secret that on the magic world 75% of control on the magic world is of the head of the magic book and 14% is of king Nigla and 6% was of king Dashwood and 5% is of Mavish. But the main important part and the administrative part is Teblanpur in the magic world.

10

Head of the magic book

When the Aurial asked the Mavish that if you are the king of the magic book then who is the head of the magic book and how did it come in Teblanpur? Which was asked in part 7 "the golden palace". As the partition of the magic world was told by the ring and the head of the magic book ruled over 75% of the magic world which was told in part 9 "the challenging war". The Mavish was wondering and always thinking about the issue. Then he told the ring that please tell me the story of the head of the magic book and how did it come here? Then the ring told that listen:

There was a king the same Sinwat. He was a prosperous and talented man. He knows all the magic of this world. He was king of the unknown kingdom. There were a brilliant teacher and Legendre for everyone. During that time, he was also having a magic book. During the time establishment of the kingdom. The contribution was all wealthy people and common people, king, saint etc. there was a famous Tiwango. So he prayed to the nature that please lead me a world-famous magic book. After 2 years of prayer to nature, nature provided a magic book. The saint Tiwango thought that if I will teach all the magic to the king it will be so good. And he will work for the welfare of the people. So he went to the king and said to him that by my prayer to nature, nature had provided me a magic book. And the saint said that, but to study or learn the magic you will have to sacrifices your all luxurious life. You will have to give your responsibility to your minister. You will have to wear normal clothes and lead a normal life like common people. The king was ready, so the saint told him to come to him tomorrow. The saint started teaching him. In starting time, he was not able to learn but he was not able. In this magic, there was a need for full concentration. The saint continuously teaching the king. Lastly, he became talented and learned all magic. And he became head of this magic book.